THE
BIRTHPLACE

By

HENRY JAMES
1922

Double 9
BOOKS

The Birthplace

by **Henry James**

ISBN: 978-93-57271-60-8

Published by

DOUBLE 9 BOOKS

2/13-B, Ansari Road
Daryaganj, New Delhi – 110002
info@double9books.com
www.double9books.com
Tel. 011-40042856

This book is under public domain

Printed in India.

ABOUT THE AUTHOR

Henry James, an American-British author, was born on April 15, 1843, and died on February 28, 1916. He is well-known as a key transitional personality between literary realism and modernism. His novels dealt with the social and marital interplay between Americans, English people, and continental Europeans. Author Henry James was nominated for the Nobel Prize for English Literature. His novel, "The Turn of the Screw," is regarded as one of the most analyzed and ambiguous ghost stories in the English language. The Wings of the Dove (1902), The Ambassadors (1903), and The Golden Bowl (1904) were James's three most significant novels. Henry James was the author of 20 novels, 112 tales, 12 plays, several volumes of travel and criticism, and a great deal of literary journalism. A master of prose fiction from the beginning, he practiced it as a fertile innovator, enlarged the form, and placed upon it his own stamp. The Ambassadors is the first in a series of three novels by Henry James, published between 1901 and 1914, dealing with the subject of an heiress doomed to die by illness. This novel avoids its cliché subject by focusing on the characters surrounding the unfortunate young woman.

CONTENTS

I

It seemed to them at first, the offer, too good to be true, and their friend's letter, addressed to them to feel, as he said, the ground, to sound them as to inclinations and possibilities, had almost the effect of a brave joke at their expense. Their friend, Mr. Grant-Jackson, a highly preponderant pushing person, great in discussion and arrangement, abrupt in overture, unexpected, if not perverse, in attitude, and almost equally acclaimed and objected to in the wide midland region to which he had taught, as the phrase was, the size of his foot—their friend had launched his bolt quite out of the blue and had thereby so shaken them as to make them fear almost more than hope. The place had fallen vacant by the death of one of the two ladies, mother and daughter, who had discharged its duties for fifteen years; the daughter was staying on alone, to accommodate, but had found, though extremely mature, an opportunity of marriage that involved retirement, and the question of the new incumbents was not a little pressing. The want thus determined was of a united couple of some sort, of the right sort, a pair of educated and competent sisters possibly preferred, but a married pair having its advantages if other qualifications were marked. Applicants, candidates, besiegers of the door of every one supposed to have a voice in the matter, were already beyond counting, and Mr. Grant-Jackson, who was in his way diplomatic and whose voice, though not perhaps of the loudest, possessed notes of insistence, had found his preference fixing itself on some person or brace of persons who had been decent and dumb. The Gedges appeared to have struck him as waiting in silence—though absolutely, as happened, no busy body had brought them, far away in the North, a hint either of bliss or of danger; and the happy spell, for the rest, had obviously been wrought in him by a remembrance which, though now scarcely fresh, had never before borne any such fruit.

Morris Gedge had for a few years, as a young man, carried on a small private school of the order known as preparatory, and had happened then to receive under his roof the small son of the great man, who was not at that time so great. The little boy, during an absence of his parents from England, had been dangerously ill, so dangerously that they had been recalled in haste, though with inevitable delays, from a far country—they had gone to America, with the whole continent and the great sea to cross again—and had got back to find the child saved, but saved, as couldn't help coming to light, by the extreme devotion and perfect judgement of Mrs. Gedge. Without children of her own she had particularly attached herself to this tiniest and tenderest of her husband's pupils, and they had both dreaded as a dire disaster the injury to their little enterprise that would be caused by their losing him. Nervous anxious sensitive persons, with a pride—as they were for that matter well aware—above their position, never, at the best, to be anything but dingy, they had nursed him in terror and had brought him through in exhaustion. Exhaustion, as befell, had thus overtaken them early and had for one reason and another managed to assert itself as their permanent portion. The little boy's death would, as they said, have done for them, yet his recovery hadn't saved them; with which it was doubtless also part of a shy but stiff candour in them that they didn't regard themselves as having in a more indirect manner laid up treasure. Treasure was not to be, in any form whatever, of their dreams or of their waking sense; and the years that followed had limped under their weight, had now and then rather grievously stumbled, had even barely escaped laying them in the dust. The school hadn't prospered, had but dwindled to a close. Gedge's health had failed and still more every sign in him of a capacity to publish himself as practical. He had tried several things, he had tried many, but the final appearance was of their having tried him not less. They mostly, at the time I speak of, were trying his successors, while he found himself, with an effect of dull felicity that had come in this case from the mere postponement of change, in charge of the grey town-library of Blackport-on-Dwindle, all granite, fog and female fiction. This was a situation in which his general intelligence—admittedly his strong point—was doubtless imaged, around him, as feeling less of a strain than that mastery of particulars in which he was recognised as weak.

It was at Blackport-on-Dwindle that the silver shaft reached and pierced him; it was as an alternative to dispensing dog's-eared volumes the very titles of which, on the lips of innumerable glib girls, were a challenge to his nerves, that the wardenship of so different a temple presented itself. The stipend named exceeded little the slim wage at present paid him, but even had it been less the interest and the honour would have struck him as determinant. The shrine at which he was to preside—though he had always lacked occasion to approach it—figured to him as the most sacred known to the steps of men, the early home of the supreme poet, the Mecca of the English-speaking race. The tears came into his eyes sooner still than into his wife's while he looked about with her at their actual narrow prison, so grim with enlightenment, so ugly with industry, so turned away from any dream, so intolerable to any taste. He felt as if a window had opened into a great green woodland, a woodland that had a name all glorious, immortal, that was peopled with vivid figures, each of them renowned, and that gave out a murmur, deep as the sound of the sea, which was the rustle in forest shade of all the poetry, the beauty, the colour of life. It would be prodigious that of this transfigured world *he* should keep the key. No—he couldn›t believe it, not even when Isabel, at sight of his face, came and helpfully kissed him. He shook his head with a strange smile. "We shan't get it. Why should we? It's perfect."

"If we don't he'll simply have been cruel; which is impossible when he has waited all this time to be kind." Mrs. Gedge did believe—she *would*; since the wide doors of the world of poetry had suddenly pushed back for them it was in the form of poetic justice that they were first to know it. She had her faith in their patron; it was sudden, but now complete. "He remembers—that's all; and that's our strength."

"And what's *his*?" Gedge asked. "He may want to put us through, but that's a different thing from being able. What are our special advantages?"

"Well, that we're just the thing." Her knowledge of the needs of the case was as yet, thanks to scant information, of the vaguest, and she had never, more than her husband, stood on the sacred spot; but she saw herself waving a nicely-gloved hand over a collection of remarkable objects and saying to a compact crowd of gaping awestruck persons: "And now, please, *this* way.» She even heard herself meeting with promptness and decision an occasional inquiry from a visitor in whom audacity had prevailed over awe. She had once been with a cousin, years before, to a great northern castle, and that was the way the housekeeper had taken them round. And it was not moreover, either, that she thought of herself as a housekeeper: she was well above that, and the wave of her hand wouldn't fail to be such as to show it. This and much else she summed up as she answered her mate. "Our special advantages are that you're a gentleman."

"Oh!" said Gedge as if he had never thought of it, and yet as if too it were scarce worth thinking of.

"I see it all," she went on; "they've *had* the vulgar—they find they don›t do. We›re poor and we›re modest, but any one can see what we are.»

Gedge wondered. "Do you mean——?" More modest than she, he didn't know quite what she meant.

"We're refined. We know how to speak."

"Do we?"—he still, suddenly, wondered.

But she was from the first surer of everything than he; so that when a few weeks more had elapsed and the shade of uncertainty—though it was only a shade—had grown almost to sicken him, her triumph was to come with the news that they were fairly named. "We're on poor pay, though we manage"—she had at the present juncture contended for her point. "But we're highly cultivated, and for them to get *that*, don't you see? without getting too much with it in the way of pretensions and demands, must be precisely their dream. We've no social position, but we don't *mind* that we haven›t, do we? a bit; which is because we know the difference between realities and shams. We hold to reality, and that gives us common sense, which the vulgar have less than anything and which yet must be wanted there, after all, as well as anywhere else."

Her companion followed her, but musingly, as if his horizon had within a few moments grown so great that he was almost lost in it and required a new orientation. The shining spaces surrounded him; the association alone gave a nobler arch to the sky. "Allow that we hold also a little to the romance. It seems to me that that's the beauty. We've missed it all our life, and now it's come. We shall be at headquarters for it. We shall have our fill of it."

She looked at his face, at the effect in it of these prospects, and her own lighted as if he had suddenly grown handsome. "Certainly—we shall live as in a fairy-tale. But what I mean is that we shall give, in a way—and so gladly— quite as much as we get. With all the rest of it we're for instance neat." Their letter had come to them at breakfast, and she picked a fly out of the butter-dish. "It's the way we'll *keep* the place»—with which she removed from the sofa to the top of the cottage-piano a tin of biscuits that had refused to squeeze into the cupboard. At Blackport they were in lodgings—of the lowest description, she had been known to declare with a freedom felt by Blackport to be slightly invidious. The Birthplace—and that itself, after such a life, was exaltation— wouldn't be lodgings, since a house close beside it was set apart for the warden, a house joining on to it as a sweet old parsonage is often annexed to a quaint old church. It would all together be their home, and such a home as would make a little world that they would never want to leave. She dwelt on the gain, for that matter, to their income; as obviously, though the salary was not a change for the better, the house given them would make all the difference. He assented to this, but absently, and she was almost impatient at the range of his thoughts. It was as if something for him—the very swarm of them—veiled the view; and he presently of himself showed what it was.

"What I can't get over is its being such a man—!" He almost, from inward emotion, broke down.

"Such a man——?"

"Him, *him*, HIM——!" It was too much.

"Grant-Jackson? Yes, it's a surprise, but one sees how he has been meaning, all the while, the right thing by us."

"I mean *Him*," Gedge returned more coldly; "our becoming familiar and intimate—for that's what it will come to. We shall just live with Him."

"Of course—it *is* the beauty.» And she added quite gaily: «The more we do the more we shall love Him.»

"No doubt—but it's rather awful. The more we *know* Him,» Gedge reflected, «the more we shall love Him. We don't as yet, you see, know Him so very tremendously."

"We do so quite as well, I imagine, as the sort of people they've had. And that probably isn't—unless you care, as we do—so awfully necessary. For there are the facts."

"Yes—there are the facts."

"I mean the principal ones. They're all that the people—the people who come—want."

"Yes—they must be all *they* want.»

"So that they're all that those who've been in charge have needed to know."

"Ah," he said as if it were a question of honour, "we must know everything."

She cheerfully acceded: she had the merit, he felt, of keeping the case within bounds. "Everything. But about him personally," she added, "there isn't, is there? so very very much."

"More, I believe, than there used to be. They've made discoveries."

It was a grand thought. "Perhaps *we* shall make some!»

"Oh I shall be content to be a little better up in what has been done." And his eyes rested on a shelf of books, half of which, little worn but much faded, were of the florid "gift" order and belonged to the house. Of those among them that were his own most were common specimens of the reference sort, not excluding an old Bradshaw and a catalogue of the town-library. "We've not even a Set of our own. Of the Works," he explained in quick repudiation of the sense, perhaps more obvious, in which she might have taken it.

As a proof of their scant range of possessions this sounded almost abject, till the painful flush with which they met on the admission melted presently into a different glow. It was just for that kind of poorness that their new situation was, by its intrinsic charm, to console them. And Mrs. Gedge had a happy thought. "Wouldn't the Library more or less have them?"

"Oh no, we've nothing of that sort: for what do you take us?" This, however, was but the play of Gedge's high spirits: the form both depression and exhilaration most frequently took with him being a bitterness on the subject of the literary taste of Blackport. No one was so deeply acquainted with it. It acted with him in fact as so lurid a sign of the future that the charm of the thought of removal was sharply enhanced by the prospect of escape from it. The institution he served didn't of course deserve the particular reproach into which his irony had flowered; and indeed if the several Sets in which the Works were present were a trifle dusty, the dust was a little his own fault. To make up for that now he had the vision of immediately giving his time to the study of them; he saw himself indeed, inflamed with a new passion, earnestly commenting and collating. Mrs. Gedge, who had suggested that, till their move should come, they ought to read Him regularly of an evening—certain as they were to do it still more when in closer quarters with Him—Mrs. Gedge felt also, in her degree, the spell; so that the very happiest time of their anxious life was perhaps to have been the series of lamplight hours, after supper, in which, alternately taking the book, they declaimed, they almost performed, their beneficent author. He became speedily more than their author—their personal friend, their universal light, their final authority and divinity. Where in the world, they were already asking themselves, would they have been without Him? By the time their appointment arrived in form their relation to Him had immensely developed. It was amusing to Morris Gedge that he had so lately blushed for his ignorance, and he made this remark to his wife during the last hour they were able to give their study before proceeding, across half the country, to the scene of their romantic future. It was as if, in deep close throbs, in cool after-waves that broke of a sudden and bathed his mind, all possession and comprehension and sympathy, all the truth and the life and the story, had come to him, and come, as the newspapers said, to stay. "It's absurd," he didn't hesitate to say, "to talk of our not 'knowing.' So far as we don't it's because we're dunces. He's *in* the thing, over His ears, and the more we get into it the more we›re with Him. I seem to myself at any rate," he declared, "to *see* Him in it as if He were painted on the wall.»

"Oh *doesn't* one rather, the dear thing? And don›t you feel where it is?» Mrs. Gedge finely asked. «We see Him because we love Him—that›s what we do. How can we not, the old darling—with what He's doing for us? There's no light"—she had a sententious turn—"like true affection."

"Yes, I suppose that's it. And yet," her husband mused, "I see, confound me, the faults."

"That's because you're so critical. You see them, but you don't mind them. You see them, but you forgive them. You mustn't mention them *there*. We shan't, you know, be there for *that*."

"Dear no!" he laughed: "we'll chuck out any one who hints at them."

II

If the sweetness of the preliminary months had been great, great too, though almost excessive as agitation, was the wonder of fairly being housed with Him, of treading day and night in the footsteps He had worn, of touching the objects, or at all events the surfaces, the substances, over which His hands had played, which His arms, His shoulders had rubbed, of breathing the air—or something not too unlike it—in which His voice had sounded. They had had a little at first their bewilderments, their disconcertedness; the place was both humbler and grander than they had exactly prefigured, more at once of a cottage and of a museum, a little more archaically bare and yet a little more richly official. But the sense was strong with them that the point of view, for the inevitable ease of the connexion, patiently, indulgently awaited them; in addition to which, from the first evening, after closing-hour, when the last blank pilgrim had gone, the mere spell, the mystic presence—as if they had had it quite to themselves—were all they could have desired. They had received, at Grant-Jackson's behest and in addition to a table of instructions and admonitions by the number and in some particulars by the nature of which they found themselves slightly depressed, various little guides, manuals, travellers' tributes, literary memorials and other catch-penny publications; which, however, were to be for the moment swallowed up in the interesting episode of the induction or initiation appointed for them in advance at the hands of several persons whose relation to the establishment was, as superior to their own, still more official, and at those in especial of one of the ladies who had for so many years borne the brunt. About the instructions from above, about the shilling books and the well-known facts and the full-blown legend, the supervision, the subjection, the submission, the view as of a cage in which he should circulate and a groove in which he should slide, Gedge had preserved a certain play of mind; but all power of reaction appeared suddenly to desert him in the presence of his so visibly competent predecessor and as an effect of her good offices. He had not the resource, enjoyed by his wife, of seeing himself, with impatience, attired in black silk of a make characterised by just the right shade of austerity; so that this firm smooth expert and consummately respectable middle-aged person had him somehow, on the whole ground, completely at her mercy.

It was evidently something of a rueful moment when, as a lesson—she being for the day or two still in the field—he accepted Miss Putchin's suggestion of "going round" with her and with the successive squads of visitors she was there to deal with. He appreciated her method—he saw there had to be one; he admired her as succinct and definite; for there were the facts, as his wife had said at Blackport, and they were to be disposed of in the time; yet he felt a very little boy as he dangled, more than once, with Mrs. Gedge, at the tail of the human comet. The idea had been that they should by this attendance more fully embrace the possible accidents and incidents, so to put it, of the relation to the great public in which they were to find themselves; and the poor man's excited perception of the great public rapidly became such as to resist any diversion meaner than that of the admirable manner of their guide. It wandered from his gaping companions to that of the priestess in black silk, whom he kept asking himself if either he or Isabel could hope by any possibility ever remotely to resemble; then it bounded restlessly back to the numerous persons who revealed to him as it had never yet been revealed the happy power of the simple to hang upon the lips of the wise. The great thing seemed to be—and quite surprisingly—that the business was easy and the strain, which as a strain they had feared, moderate; so that he might have been puzzled, had he fairly caught himself in the act, by his recognising as the last effect of the impression an odd absence of the power really to rest in it, an agitation deep within him that vaguely threatened to grow. "It isn't, you see, so very complicated," the black silk lady seemed to throw off, with everything else, in her neat crisp cheerful way; in spite of which he already, the very first time—that is after several parties had been in and out and up and down—went so far as to wonder if there weren't more in it than she imagined. She was, so to speak, kindness itself—was all encouragement and reassurance; but it was just her slightly coarse redolence of these very things that, on repetition, before they parted, dimmed a little, as he felt, the light of his acknowledging smile. This again she took for a symptom of some pleading weakness in him—he could never be as brave as she; so that she wound up with a few pleasant words from the very depth of her experience. "You'll get into it, never fear—it will *come*; and then you'll feel as if you had never done anything else." He was afterwards to know that, on the spot, at this moment, he must have begun to wince a little at such a menace; that he might come to feel as if he had never done anything but what Miss Putchin did loomed for him, in germ, as a penalty to pay. The support she offered, none the less, continued to strike him; she put the whole thing on so sound a basis when she said: "You see they're so nice about it—they take such an interest. And they never do a thing they shouldn't. That was always every thing to mother and me." "They," Gedge had already noticed, referred constantly and hugely, in the good woman's talk, to the millions who shuffled through the house; the pronoun in question was for ever on her lips, the hordes it represented filled her consciousness, the addition of their numbers ministered to her glory. Mrs. Gedge promptly fell in. "It must be indeed delightful to see the effect on so many and to feel that one may perhaps do something to make it—well, permanent." But he was kept silent by his becoming more sharply aware that this was a new view, for him, of the reference made, that he had never thought of the quality of the place as derived from Them, but from Somebody Else, and that They, in short, seemed to have got into the way of crowding Him out. He found himself even a little resenting this for Him—which perhaps had something to do with the slightly invidious cast of his next inquiry.

"And are They always, as one might say—a—stupid?"

"Stupid!" She stared, looking as if no one *could* be such a thing in such a connexion. No one had ever been anything but neat and cheerful and fluent, except to be attentive and unobjectionable and, so far as was possible, American.

"What I mean is," he explained, "is there any perceptible proportion that take an interest in Him?"

His wife stepped on his toe; she deprecated levity.

But his mistake fortunately was lost on their friend.

"That's just why they come, that they take such an interest. I sometimes think they take more than about anything else in the world." With which Miss Putchin looked about at the place. "It *is* pretty, don›t you think, the way they›ve got it now?» This, Gedge saw, was a different "They"; it applied to the powers that were—the people who had appointed him, the governing, visiting Body, in respect to which he was afterwards to remark to Mrs. Gedge that a fellow—it was the difficulty—didn't know "where to have her." His wife, at a loss, questioned at that moment the necessity of having her anywhere, and he said, good-humouredly, "Of course; it's all right." He was in fact content enough with the last touches their friend had given the picture. "There are many who know all about it when they come, and the Americans often are tremendously up. Mother and me really enjoyed"—it was her only slip—"the interest of the Americans. We've sometimes had ninety a day, and all wanting to see and hear everything. But you'll work them off; you'll see the way—it's all experience." She came back for his comfort to that. She came back also to other things: she did justice to the considerable class who arrived positive and primed. "There are those who know more about it than you do. But *that* only comes from their interest."

"Who know more about what?" Gedge inquired.

"Why about the place. I mean they have their ideas—of what everything is, and *where* it is, and what it isn›t and where it *should* be. They do ask questions,» she said, yet not so much in warning as in the complacency of being herself seasoned and sound; "and they're down on you when they think you go wrong. As if you ever could! You know too much," she astutely smiled; "or you *will*."

"Oh you mustn't know *too* much, must you?» And Gedge now smiled as well. He knew, he thought, what he meant.

"Well, you must know as much as anybody else. I claim at any rate that I do," Miss Putchin declared. "They never really caught me out."

"I'm very certain of *that*"—and Mrs. Gedge had an elation almost personal.

"Surely," he said, "I don't want to be caught out." She rejoined that in such a case he would have *Them* down on him, and he saw that this time she meant the powers above. It quickened his sense of all the elements that were to reckon with, yet he felt at the same time that the powers above were not what he should most fear. "I'm glad," he observed, "that they ever ask questions; but I happened to notice, you know, that no one did to-day."

"Then you missed several—and no loss. There were three or four put to me too silly to remember. But of course they mostly *are* silly.»

"You mean the questions?"

She laughed with all her cheer. "Yes, sir; I don't mean the answers."

Whereupon, for a moment snubbed and silent, he felt like one of the crowd. Then it made him slightly vicious. "I didn't know but you meant the people in general—till I remembered that I'm to understand from you that *they're* wise, only occasionally breaking down.»

It wasn't really till then, he thought, that she lost patience; and he had had, much more than he meant no doubt, a cross-questioning air. "You'll see for yourself." Of which he was sure enough. He was in fact so ready to take this that she came round to full accommodation, put it frankly that every now and then they broke out—not the silly, oh no, the intensely inquiring. "We've had quite lively discussions, don't you know, about well-known points. They want it all *their* way, and I know the sort that are going to as soon as I see them. That›s one of the things you do—you get to know the sorts. And if it's what you're afraid of—their taking you up," she was further gracious enough to say, "you needn't mind a bit. What *do* they know, after all, when for us it›s our life? I›ve never moved an inch, because, you see, I shouldn›t have been here if I didn't know where I was. No more will *you* be a year hence—you know what I mean, putting it impossibly—if you don›t. I expect you do, in spite of your fancies.» And she dropped once more to bed-rock. «There are the facts. Otherwise where would any of us be? That's all you've got to go upon. A person, however cheeky, can't have them *his* way just because he takes it into his head. There can only be *one* way, and,» she gaily added as she took leave of them, «I›m sure it›s quite enough!»

III

Gedge not only assented eagerly—one way *was* quite enough if it were the right one—but repeated it, after this conversation, at odd moments, several times over to his wife. «There can only be one way, one way,» he continued to remark—though indeed much as if it were a joke; till she asked him how many more he supposed she wanted. He failed to answer this question, but resorted to another repetition. "There are the facts, the facts," which perhaps, however, he kept a little more to himself, sounding it at intervals in different parts of the house. Mrs. Gedge was full of comment on their clever introductress, though not restrictively save in the matter of her speech, "Me and mother," and a general tone—which certainly was not their sort of thing. "I don't know," he said, "perhaps it comes with the place, since speaking in immortal verse doesn't seem to come. It must be, one seems to see, one thing or the other. I daresay that in a few months I shall also be at it—'me and the wife.'"

"Why not 'me and the missus' at once?" Mrs. Gedge resentfully inquired. "I don't think," she observed at another time, "that I quite know what's the matter with you."

"It's only that I'm excited, awfully excited—as I don't see how one can't be. You wouldn't have a fellow drop into this berth as into an appointment at the Post Office. Here on the spot it goes to my head—how can that be helped? But we shall live into it, and perhaps," he said with an implication of the other possibility that was doubtless but part of his fine ecstasy, "we shall live through it." The place acted on his imagination—how, surely, shouldn't it? And his imagination acted on his nerves, and these things together, with the general vividness and the new and complete immersion, made rest for him almost impossible, so that he could scarce go to bed at night and even during the first week more than once rose in the small hours to move about, up and down, with his lamp—standing, sitting, listening, wondering, in the stillness, as if positively to recover some echo, to surprise some secret, of the *genius loci*. He couldn't have explained it—and didn't in fact need to explain it, at least to himself, since the impulse simply held him and shook him; but the time after closing, the time above all after the people—Them, as he felt himself on the way habitually to put it, predominant, insistent, all in the foreground—brought him, or ought to have brought him, he seemed to see, nearer to the enshrined Presence, enlarging the opportunity for communion and intensifying the sense of it. These nightly prowls, as he called them, were disquieting to his wife, who had no disposition to share in them, speaking with decision of the whole place as just the place to be forbidding after dark. She rejoiced in the distinctness, contiguous though it was, of their own little residence, where she trimmed the lamp and stirred the fire and heard the kettle sing, repairing the while the omissions of the small domestic who slept out; she foresaw her self, with some promptness, drawing rather sharply the line between her own precinct and that in which the great spirit might walk. It would be with them, the great spirit, all day—even if indeed on her making that remark, and in just that form, to her husband, he replied with a queer "But will he though?" And she vaguely imaged the development of a domestic antidote after a while, precisely, in the shape of curtains more markedly drawn and everything most modern and lively, tea, "patterns," the newspapers, the female fiction itself that they had reacted against at Blackport, quite defiantly cultivated.

These possibilities, however, were all right, as her companion said it was, all the first autumn—they had arrived at summer's end; and he might have been more than content with a special set of his own that he had access to from behind, passing out of their low door for the few steps between it and the Birthplace. With his lamp ever so carefully guarded and his nursed keys that made him free of treasures, he crossed the dusky interval so often that she began to qualify it as a habit that "grew." She spoke of it almost as if he had taken to drink, and he humoured that view of it by allowing the cup to be strong. This had been in truth altogether his immediate sense of it; strange and deep for him the spell of silent sessions before familiarity and, to some small extent, disappointment had set in. The exhibitional side of the establishment had struck him, even on arrival, as qualifying too much its character; he scarce knew what he might best have looked for, but the three or four rooms bristled overmuch, in the garish light of day, with busts and relics, not even ostensibly always *His*, old prints and old editions, old objects fashioned in His likeness, furniture "of the time" and autographs of celebrated worshippers. In the quiet hours and the deep dusk, none the less, under the play of the shifted lamp and that of his own emotion, these things too recovered their advantage, ministered to the mystery, or at all events to the impression, seemed consciously to offer themselves as personal to the poet. Not one of them was really or unchallengeably so, but they had somehow, through long association, got, as Gedge always phrased it, into the secret, and it was about the secret he asked them while he restlessly wandered. It wasn't till months had elapsed that he found how little they had to tell him, and he was quite at his ease with them when he knew they were by no means where his sensibility had first placed them. They were as out of it as he; only, to do them justice, they had made him immensely feel. And still, too, it was not they who had done that most, since his sentiment had gradually cleared itself to deep, to deeper refinements.

The Holy of Holies of the Birthplace was the low, the sublime Chamber of Birth, sublime because, as the Americans usually said—unlike the natives they mostly found words—it was so pathetic; and pathetic because it was—well, really nothing else in the world that one could name, number or measure. It was as empty as a shell of which the kernel has withered, and contained neither busts nor prints nor early copies; it contained only the Fact—*the* Fact itself— which, as he stood sentient there at midnight, our friend, holding his breath, allowed to sink into him. He *had* to take it as the place where the spirit would most walk and where He would therefore be most to be met, with possibilities of recognition and reciprocity. He hadn't, most probably—*He* hadn›t—much inhabited the room, as men weren›t apt, as a rule, to convert to their later use and involve in their wider fortune the scene itself of their nativity. But as there were moments when, in the conflict of theories, the sole certainty surviving for the critic threatened to be that He had not—unlike other successful men— *not* been born, so Gedge, though little of a critic, clung to the square feet of space that connected themselves, however feebly, with the positive appearance. He was little of a critic—he was nothing of one; he hadn't pretended to the character before coming, nor come to pretend to it; also, luckily for him, he was seeing day by day how little use he could possibly have for it. It would be to him, the attitude of a high expert, distinctly a stumbling-block, and that he rejoiced, as the winter waned, in his ignorance, was one of the propositions he betook himself, in his odd manner, to enunciating to his wife. She denied it, for hadn't she in the first place been present, wasn't she still present, at his pious, his tireless study of everything connected with the subject?—so present that she had herself learned more about it than had ever seemed likely. Then in the second place he wasn't to proclaim on the house-tops any point at which he might be weak, for who knew, if it should get abroad that they were ignorant, what effect might be produced?——

"On the attraction"—he took her up—"of the Show?"

He had fallen into the harmless habit of speaking of the place as the "Show"; but she didn't mind this so much as to be diverted by it. "No; on the attitude of the Body. You know they're pleased with us, and I don't see why you should want to spoil it. We got in by a tight squeeze—you know we've had evidence of that, and that it was about as much as our backers could manage. But we're proving a comfort to them, and it's absurd of you to question your suitability to people who were content with the Putchins."

"I don't, my dear," he returned, "question any thing; but if I should do so it would be precisely because of the greater advantage constituted for the Putchins by the simplicity of their spirit. They were kept straight by the quality of their ignorance—which was denser even than mine. It was a mistake in us from the first to have attempted to correct or to disguise ours. We should have waited simply to become good parrots, to learn our lesson—all on the spot here, so little of it is wanted—and squawk it off."

"Ah 'squawk,' love—what a word to use about Him!"

"It isn't about Him—nothing's about Him. None of Them care tuppence about Him. The only thing They care about is this empty shell—or rather, for it isn't empty, the extraneous preposterous stuffing of it."

"Preposterous?"—he made her stare with this as he hadn't yet done.

At sight of her look, however—the gleam, as it might have been, of a queer suspicion—he bent to her kindly and tapped her cheek. "Oh it's all right. We *must* fall back on the Putchins. Do you remember what she said?—›They›ve made it so pretty now.› They *have* made it pretty, and it›s a first-rate show. It›s a first-rate show and a first-rate billet, and He was a first-rate poet, and you're a first-rate woman—to put up so sweetly, I mean, with my nonsense."

She appreciated his domestic charm and she justified that part of his tribute which concerned herself. "I don't care how much of your nonsense you talk to me, so long as you *keep* it all for me and don›t treat *Them* to it.»

"The pilgrims? No," he conceded—"it isn't fair to Them. They mean well."

"What complaint have we after all to make of Them so long as They don't break off bits—as They used, Miss Putchin told us, so awfully—in order to conceal them about Their Persons? She broke Them at least of that."

"Yes," Gedge mused again; "I wish awfully she hadn't!"

"You'd like the relics destroyed, removed? That's all that's wanted!"

"There *are* no relics.»

"There won't be any *soon*—unless you take care." But he was already laughing, and the talk wasn't dropped without his having patted her once more. An impression or two nevertheless remained with her from it, as he saw from a question she asked him on the morrow. "What did you mean yesterday about Miss Putchin's simplicity—its keeping her 'straight'? Do you mean mentally?"

Her "mentally" was rather portentous, but he practically confessed. "Well, it kept her up. I mean," he amended, laughing, "it kept her down."

It was really as if she had been a little uneasy. "You consider there's a danger of your being affected? You know what I mean—of its going to your head. You do know," she insisted as he said nothing. "Through your caring for him so. You'd certainly be right in that case about its having been a mistake for you to plunge so deep." And then as his listening without reply, though with his look a little sad for her, might have denoted that, allowing for extravagance of statement, he saw there was something in it: "Give up your prowls. Keep it for daylight. Keep it for *Them*."

"Ah," he smiled, "if one could! My prowls," he added, "are what I most enjoy. They're the only time, as I've told you before, that I'm really with *Him*. Then I don't see the place. He isn't the place."

"I don't care for what you 'don't see,'" she returned with vivacity; "the question is of what you do see."

Well, if it was, he waited before meeting it. "Do you know what I sometimes do?" And then as she waited too: "In the Birthroom there, when I look in late, I often put out my light. That makes it better."

"Makes what——?"

"Everything."

"What is it then you see in the dark?"

"Nothing!" said Morris Gedge.

"And what's the pleasure of that?"

"Well, what the American ladies say. It's so fascinating!"

IV

The autumn was brisk, as Miss Putchin had told them it would be, but business naturally fell off with the winter months and the short days. There was rarely an hour indeed without a call of some sort, and they were never allowed to forget that they kept the shop in all the world, as they might say, where custom was least fluctuating. The seasons told on it, as they tell on travel, but no other influence, consideration or convulsion to which the population of the globe is exposed. This population, never exactly in simultaneous hordes, but in a full swift and steady stream, passed through the smoothly-working mill and went, in its variety of degrees duly impressed and edified, on its artless way. Gedge gave himself up, with much ingenuity of spirit, to trying to keep in relation with it; having even at moments, in the early time, glimpses of the chance that the impressions gathered from so rare an opportunity for contact with the general mind might prove as interesting as anything else in the connexion. Types, classes, nationalities, manners, diversities of behaviour, modes of seeing, feeling, of expression, would pass before him and become for him, after a fashion, the experience of an untravelled man. His journeys had been short and saving, but poetic justice again seemed inclined to work for him in placing him just at the point in all Europe perhaps where the confluence of races was thickest. The theory at any rate carried him on, operating helpfully for the term of his anxious beginnings and gilding in a manner—it was the way he characterised the case to his wife—the somewhat stodgy gingerbread of their daily routine. They hadn't known many people and their visiting-list was small—which made it again poetic justice that they should be visited on such a scale. They dressed and were at home, they were under arms and received, and except for the offer of refreshment—and Gedge had his view that there would eventually be a *buffet* farmed out to a great firm—their hospitality would have made them princely if mere hospitality ever did. Thus they were launched, and it was interesting; so that from having been ready to drop, originally, with fatigue they emerged as even-winded and strong in the legs as if they had had an Alpine holiday. This experience, Gedge opined, also represented, as a gain, a like seasoning of the spirit—by which he meant a certain command of impenetrable patience.

The patience was needed for the particular feature of the ordeal that, by the time the lively season was with them again, had disengaged itself as the sharpest—the immense assumption of veracities and sanctities, of the general soundness of the legend, with which every one arrived. He was well provided certainly for meeting it, and he gave all he had, yet he had sometimes the sense of a vague resentment on the part of his pilgrims at his not ladling out their fare with a bigger spoon. An irritation had begun to grumble in him during the comparatively idle months of winter when a pilgrim would turn up singly. The pious individual, entertained for the half-hour, had occasionally seemed to offer him the promise of beguilement or the semblance of a personal relation; it came back again to the few pleasant calls he had received in the course of a life almost void of social amenity. Sometimes he liked the person, the face, the speech: an educated man, a gentleman, not one of the herd; a graceful woman, vague, accidental, unconscious of him, but making him wonder, while he hovered, who she was. These chances represented for him light yearnings and faint flutters; they acted indeed within him to a special, an extraordinary tune. He would have liked to talk with such stray companions, to talk with them *really*, to talk with them as he might have talked had he met them where he couldn't meet them—at dinner, in the "world," on a visit at a country-house. Then he could have said—and about the shrine and the idol always—things he couldn't say now. The form in which his irritation first came to him was that of his feeling obliged to say to them—to the single visitor, even when sympathetic, quite as to the gaping group—the particular things, a dreadful dozen or so, that they expected. If he had thus arrived at characterising these things as dreadful the reason touched the very point that, for a while turning everything over, he kept dodging, not facing, trying to ignore. The point was that he was on his way to become two quite different persons, the public and the private—as to which it would somehow have to be managed that these persons should live together. He was splitting into halves, unmistakably—he who, whatever else he had been, had at least always been so entire and in his way so solid. One of the halves, or perhaps even, since the split promised to be rather unequal, one of the quarters, was the keeper, the showman, the priest of the idol; the other piece was the poor unsuccessful honest man he had always been.

There were moments when he recognised this primary character as he had never done before; when he in fact quite shook in his shoes at the idea that it perhaps had in reserve some supreme assertion of its identity. It was honest, verily, just by reason of the possibility. It was poor and unsuccessful because here it was just on the verge of quarrelling with its bread and butter. Salvation would be of course—the salvation of the showman—rigidly to *keep* it on the verge; not to let it, in other words, overpass by an inch. He might count on this, he said to himself, if there weren›t any public—if there weren›t thousands of people demanding of him what he was paid for. He saw the approach of the stage at which they would affect him, the thousands of people—and perhaps even more the earnest individual—as coming really to see if he were earning his wage. Wouldn't he soon begin to fancy them in league with the Body, practically deputed by it—given, no doubt, a kindled suspicion—to look in and report observations? It was the way he broke down with the lonely pilgrim that led to his first heart-searchings—broke down as to the courage required for damping an uncritical faith. What they all most wanted was to feel that everything was "just as it was"; only the shock of having to part with that vision was greater than any individual could bear unsupported. The bad moments were upstairs in the Birthroom, for here the forces pressing on the very edge assumed a dire intensity. The mere expression of eye, all-credulous, omnivorous and fairly moistening in the act, with which many persons gazed about, might eventually make it difficult for him to remain fairly civil. Often they came in pairs—sometimes one had come before-—and then they explained to each other. He in that case never corrected; he listened, for the lesson of listening: after which he would remark to his wife that there was no end to what he was learning. He saw that if he should really ever break down it would be with her he would begin. He had given her hints and digs enough, but she was so inflamed with appreciation that she either didn't feel them or pretended not to understand.

This was the greater complication that, with the return of the spring and the increase of the public, her services were more required. She took the field with him from an early hour; she was present with the party above while he kept an eye, and still more an ear, on the party below; and how could he know, he asked himself, what she might say to them and what she might suffer *Them* to say—or in other words, poor wretches, to believe—while removed from his control? Some day or other, and before too long, he couldn›t but think, he must have the matter out with her—the matter, namely, of the *morality* of their position. The morality of women was special—he was getting lights on that. Isabel›s conception of her office was to cherish and enrich the legend. It was already, the legend, very taking, but what was she there for but to make it more so? She certainly wasn't there to chill any natural piety. If it was all in the air—all in their "eye," as the vulgar might say—that He *had* been born in the Birthroom, where was the value of the sixpences they took? where the equivalent they had engaged to supply? "Oh dear, yes—just about *here*"; and she must tap the place with her foot. "Altered? Oh dear, no—save in a few trifling particulars; you see the place—and isn't that just the charm of it?—quite as *He* saw it. Very poor and homely, no doubt; but that's just what's so wonderful." He didn't want to hear her, and yet he didn't want to give her her head; he didn't want to make difficulties or to snatch the bread from her mouth. But he must none the less give her a warning before they had gone *too* far. That was the way, one evening in June, he put it to her; the affluence, with the finest weather, having lately been of the largest and the crowd all day fairly gorged with the story. «We mustn›t, you know, go *too* far.»

The odd thing was that she had now ceased even to be conscious of what troubled him—she was so launched in her own career. "Too far for what?"

"To save our immortal souls. We mustn't, love, tell too many lies."

She looked at him with dire reproach. "Ah now are you going to begin again?"

"I never *have* begun; I haven›t wanted to worry you. But, you know, we don›t know anything about it.» And then as she stared, flushing: «About His having been born up there. About anything really. Not the least little scrap that would weigh in any other connexion as evidence. So don't rub it in so."

"Rub it in how?"

"That He *was* born——» But at sight of her face he only sighed. «Oh dear, oh dear!»

"Don't you think," she replied cuttingly, "that He was born anywhere?"

He hesitated—it was such an edifice to shake. "Well, we don't know. There's very little *to* know. He covered His tracks as no other human being has ever done.»

She was still in her public costume and hadn't taken off the gloves she made a point of wearing as a part of that uniform; she remembered how the rustling housekeeper in the Border castle, on whom she had begun by modelling herself, had worn them. She seemed official and slightly distant. "To cover His tracks He must have had to exist. Have we got to give *that* up?»

"No, I don't ask you to give it up *yet*. But there's very little to go upon."

"And is that what I'm to tell Them in return for everything?"

Gedge waited—he walked about. The place was doubly still after the bustle of the day, and the summer evening rested on it as a blessing, making it, in its small state and ancientry, mellow and sweet. It was good to be there and it would be good to stay. At the same time there was something incalculable in the effect on one's nerves of the great gregarious density. This was an attitude that had nothing to do with degrees and shades, the attitude of wanting all or nothing. And you couldn't talk things over with it. You could only do that with friends, and then but in cases where you were sure the friends wouldn't betray you. "Couldn't you adopt," he replied at last, "a slightly more discreet method? What we can say is that things have been *said*; that's all we have to do with. 'And is this really'—when they jam their umbrellas into the floor—'the very *spot* where He was born?' 'So it has, from a long time back, been described as being.' Couldn't one meet Them, to be decent a little, in some such way as that?"

She looked at him very hard. "Is that the way *you* meet them?»

"No; I've kept on lying—without scruple, without shame."

"Then why do you haul me up?"

"Because it has seemed to me we might, like true companions, work it out a little together."

This was not strong, he felt, as, pausing with his hands in his pockets, he stood before her; and he knew it as weaker still after she had looked at him a minute. "Morris Gedge, I propose to be *your* true companion, and I›ve come here to stay. That›s all I›ve got to say.» It was not, however, for «You had better try yourself and see,» she presently added. «Give the place, give the story away, by so much as a look, and—well, I'd allow you about nine days. Then you'd see."

He feigned, to gain time, an innocence. "They'd take it so ill?" And then as she said nothing: "They'd turn and rend me? They'd tear me to pieces?"

But she wouldn't make a joke of it. "They wouldn't *have* it, simply.»

"No—They wouldn't. That's what I say. They won't."

"You had better," she went on, "begin with Grant-Jackson. But even that isn't necessary. It would get to him, it would get to the Body, like wildfire."

"I see," said poor Gedge. And indeed for the moment he did see, while his companion followed up what she believed her advantage.

"Do you consider it's *all* a fraud?»

"Well, I grant you there was somebody. But the details are naught. The links are missing. The evidence—in particular about that room upstairs, in itself our Casa Santa—is *nil*. It was so awfully long ago." Which he knew again sounded weak.

"Of course it was awfully long ago—that's just the beauty and the interest. Tell Them, *tell* Them,» she continued, "that the evidence is *nil*, and I'll tell Them something else." She spoke it with such meaning that his face seemed to show a question, to which she was on the spot of replying, "I'll tell Them you're a——" She stopped, however, changing it. "I'll tell Them exactly the opposite. And I'll find out what you say—it won't take long—to do it. If we tell different stories *that* possibly may save us.»

"I see what you mean. It would perhaps, as an oddity, have a success of curiosity. It might become a draw. Still, They but want broad masses." And he looked at her sadly. "You're no more than one of Them."

"If it's being no more than one of Them to love it," she answered, "then I certainly am. And I'm not ashamed of my company."

"To love *what*?" said Morris Gedge.

"To love to think He was born there."

"You think too much. It's bad for you." He turned away with his chronic moan. But it was without losing what she called after him.

"I decline to let the place down." And what was there indeed to say? They *were* there to keep it up.

V

He kept it up through the summer, but with the queerest consciousness, at times, of the want of proportion between his secret rage and the spirit of those from whom the friction came. He said to himself—so sore his sensibility had grown—that They were gregariously ferocious at the very time he was seeing Them as individually mild. He said to himself that They were mild only because *he* was—he flattered himself that he was divinely so, considering what he might be; and that he should, as his wife had warned him, soon enough have news of it were he to deflect by a hair's breadth from the line traced for him. *That* was the collective fatuity—that it was capable of turning on the instant both to a general and to a particular resentment. Since the least breath of discrimination would get him the sack without mercy, it was absurd, he reflected, to speak of his discomfort as light. He was gagged, he was goaded, as in omnivorous companies he doubtless sometimes showed by a strange silent glare. They'd get him the sack for that as well, if he didn't look out; therefore wasn't it in effect ferocity when you mightn't even hold your tongue? They wouldn't let you off with silence—They insisted on your committing yourself. It was the pound of flesh—They *would* have it; so under his coat he bled. But a wondrous peace, by exception, dropped on him one afternoon at the end of August. The pressure had, as usual, been high, but it had diminished with the fall of day, and the place was empty before the hour for closing. Then it was that, within a few minutes of this hour, there presented themselves a pair of pilgrims to whom in the ordinary course he would have remarked that they were, to his regret, too late. He was to wonder afterwards why the course had at sight of the visitors—a gentleman and a lady, appealing and fairly young— shown for him as other than ordinary; the consequence sprang doubtless from something rather fine and unnameable, something for example in the tone of the young man or in the light of his eye, after hearing the statement on the subject of the hour. "Yes, we know it's late; but it's just, I'm afraid, *because* of that. We›ve had rather a notion of escaping the crowd—as I suppose you mostly have one now; and it was really on the chance of finding you alone——!"

These things the young man said before being quite admitted, and they were words any one might have spoken who hadn't taken the trouble to be punctual or who desired, a little ingratiatingly, to force the door. Gedge even guessed at the sense that might lurk in them, the hint of a special tip if the point were stretched. There were no tips, he had often thanked his stars, at the Birthplace; there was the charged fee and nothing more; everything else was out of order, to the relief of a palm not formed by nature as a scoop. Yet in spite of everything, in spite especially of the almost audible chink of the gentleman's sovereigns, which might in another case exactly have put him out, he presently found himself, in the Birthroom, access to which he had gracefully enough granted, almost treating the visit as personal and private. The reason—well, the reason would have been, if anywhere, in something naturally persuasive on the part of the couple; unless it had been rather again, in the way the young man, once he was in the place, met the caretaker's expression of face, held it a moment and seemed to wish to sound it. That they were Americans was promptly clear, and Gedge could very nearly have told what kind; he had arrived at the point of distinguishing kinds, though the difficulty might have been with him now that the case before him was rare. He saw it suddenly in the light of the golden midland evening which reached them through low old windows, saw it with a rush of feeling, unexpected and smothered, that made him a moment wish to keep it before him as a case of inordinate happiness. It made him feel old shabby poor, but he watched it no less intensely for its doing so. They were children of fortune, of the greatest, as it might seem to Morris Gedge, and they were of course lately married; the husband, smooth-faced and soft, but resolute and fine, several years older than the wife, and the wife vaguely, delicately, irregularly, but mercilessly pretty. Some how the world was theirs; they gave the person who took the sixpences at the Birthplace such a sense of the high luxury of freedom as he had never had. The thing was that the world was theirs not simply because they had money—he had seen rich people enough—but because they could in a supreme degree think and feel and say what they liked. They had a nature and a culture, a tradition, a facility of some sort—and all producing in them an effect of positive beauty—that gave a light to their liberty and an ease to their tone. These things moreover suffered nothing from the fact that they happened to be in mourning; this was probably worn for some lately-deceased opulent father—if not some delicate mother who would be sure to have been a part of the source of the beauty; and it affected Gedge, in the gathered twilight and at his odd crisis, as the very uniform of their distinction.

He couldn't quite have said afterwards by what steps the point had been reached, but it had become at the end of five minutes a part of their presence in the Birthroom, a part of the young man's look, a part of the charm of the moment, and a part above all of a strange sense within him of "Now or never!" that Gedge had suddenly, thrillingly, let himself go. He hadn't been definitely conscious of drifting to it; he had been, for that, too conscious merely of thinking how different, in all their range, were such a united couple from another united couple known to him. They were everything he and his wife weren't; this was more than anything else the first lesson of their talk. Thousands of couples of whom the same was true certainly had passed before him, but none of whom it was true with just that engaging intensity. And just *because* of their transcendent freedom; that was what, at the end of five minutes, he saw it all come back to. The husband, who had been there at some earlier time, had his impression, which he wished now to make his wife share. But he already, Gedge could see, hadn't concealed it from her. A pleasant irony in fine our friend seemed to taste in the air—he who hadn't yet felt free to taste his own.

"I think you weren't here four years ago"—that was what the young man had almost begun by remarking. Gedge liked his remembering it, liked his frankly speaking to him; all the more that he had offered, as it were, no opening. He had let them look about below and then had taken them up, but without words, without the usual showman's song, of which he would have been afraid. The visitors didn't ask for it; the young man had taken the matter out of his hands by himself dropping for the benefit of the young woman a few detached remarks. What Gedge oddly felt was that these remarks were not inconsiderate of him; he had heard others, both of the priggish order and the crude, that might have been called so. And as the young man hadn't been aided to this cognition of him as new, it already began to make for them a certain common ground. The ground became immense when the visitor presently added with a smile: "There was a good lady, I recollect, who had a great deal to say."

It was the gentleman's smile that had done it; the irony *was* there. «Ah there has been a great deal said.» And Gedge›s look at his interlocutor doubtless showed his sense of being sounded. It was extraordinary of course that a perfect stranger should have guessed the travail of his spirit, should have caught the gleam of his inner commentary. That probably leaked in spite of him out of his poor old eyes. "Much of it, in such places as this," he heard himself adding, "is of course said very irresponsibly." *Such places as this!*—he winced at the words as soon as he had uttered them.

There was no wincing, however, on the part of his pleasant companions. "Exactly so; the whole thing becomes a sort of stiff smug convention—like a dressed-up sacred doll in a Spanish church—which you're a monster if you touch."

"A monster," Gedge assented, meeting his eyes.

The young man smiled, but he thought looking at him a little harder. "A blasphemer."

"A blasphemer."

It seemed to do his visitor good—he certainly *was* looking at him harder. Detached as he was he was interested—he was at least amused. «Then you don›t claim or at any rate don›t insist——? I mean you personally.»

He had an identity for him, Gedge felt, that he couldn't have had for a Briton, and the impulse was quick in our friend to testify to this perception. "I don't insist to *you*."

The young man laughed. "It really—I assure you if I may—wouldn't do any good. I'm too awfully interested."

"Do you mean," his wife lightly inquired, "in—a—pulling it down? That's rather in what you've said to me."

"Has he said to you," Gedge intervened, though quaking a little, "that he would like to pull it down?"

She met, in her free sweetness, this appeal with such a charm! "Oh perhaps not quite the *house*——!"

"Good. You see we live on it—I mean *we* people."

The husband had laughed, but had now so completely ceased to look about him that there seemed nothing left for him but to talk avowedly with the caretaker. "I'm interested," he explained, "in what I think *the* interesting thing—or at all events the eternally tormenting one. The fact of the abysmally little that, in proportion, we know.»

"In proportion to what?" his companion asked.

"Well, to what there must have been—to what in fact there *is*—to wonder about. That's the interest; it's immense. He escapes us like a thief at night, carrying off—well, carrying off everything. And people pretend to catch Him like a flown canary, over whom you can close your hand, and put Him back in the cage. He won't *go* back; he won't *come* back. He›s not»—the young man laughed—»such a fool! It makes Him the happiest of all great men.»

He had begun by speaking to his wife, but had ended, with his friendly, his easy, his indescribable competence, for Gedge—poor Gedge who quite held his breath and who felt, in the most unexpected way, that he had somehow never been in such good society. The young wife, who for herself meanwhile had continued to look about, sighed out, smiled out—Gedge couldn't have told which—her little answer to these remarks. "It's rather a pity, you know, that He *isn't* here. I mean as Goethe›s at Weimar. For Goethe *is* at Weimar.»

"Yes, my dear; that's Goethe's bad luck. There he sticks. *This* man isn›t anywhere. I defy you to catch him.»

"Why not say, beautifully," the young woman laughed, "that, like the wind, He's everywhere?"

It wasn't of course the tone of discussion, it was the tone of pleasantry, though of better pleasantry, Gedge seemed to feel, and more within his own appreciation, than he had ever listened to; and this was precisely why the young man could go on without the effect of irritation, answering his wife but still with eyes for their companion. "I'll be hanged if He's *here!*"

It was almost as if he were taken—that is, struck and rather held—by their companion's unruffled state, which they hadn't meant to ruffle, but which suddenly presented its interest, perhaps even projected its light. The gentleman didn't know, Gedge was afterwards to say to himself, how that hypocrite was inwardly all of a tremble, how it seemed to him his fate was being literally pulled down on his head. He was trembling for the moment certainly too much to speak; abject he might be, but he didn't want his voice to have the absurdity of a quaver. And the young woman—charming creature!—still had another word. It was for the guardian of the spot, and she made it in her way delightful. They had remained in the Holy of Holies, where she had been looking for a minute, with a ruefulness just marked enough to be pretty, at the queer old floor. "Then if you say it *wasn't* in this room He was born—well, what›s the use?»

"What's the use of what?" her husband asked. "The use, you mean, of our coming here? Why the place is charming in itself. And it's also interesting," he added to Gedge, "to know how you get on."

Gedge looked at him a moment in silence, but answering the young woman first. If poor Isabel, he was thinking, could only have been like that!—not as to youth, beauty, arrangement of hair or picturesque grace of hat—these things he didn't mind; but as to sympathy, facility, light perceptive, and yet not cheap, detachment! "I don't say it wasn't—but I don't say it *was.*"

"Ah but doesn't that," she returned, "come very much to the same thing? And don't They want also to see where He had His dinner and where He had His tea?"

"They want everything," said Morris Gedge. "They want to see where He hung up His hat and where He kept His boots and where His mother boiled her pot."

"But if you don't show them——?"

"They show *me*. It's in all their little books."

"You mean," the husband asked, "that you've only to hold your tongue?"

"I try to," said Gedge.

"Well," his visitor smiled, "I see you *can*."

Gedge hesitated. "I can't."

"Oh well," said his friend, "what does it matter?"

"I do speak," he continued. "I can't sometimes not."

"Then how do you get on?"

Gedge looked at him more abjectly, to his own sense, than ever at any one—even at Isabel when she frightened him. "I don't get on. I speak," he said—"since I've spoken to *you*."

"Oh *we* shan't hurt you!" the young man reassuringly laughed.

The twilight meanwhile had sensibly thickened, the end of the visit was indicated. They turned together out of the upper room and came down the narrow stair. The words just exchanged might have been felt as producing an awkwardness which the young woman gracefully felt the impulse to dissipate. "You must rather wonder why we've come." And it was the first note for Gedge of a further awkwardness—as if he had definitely heard it make the husband's hand, in a full pocket, begin to fumble.

It was even a little awkwardly that the husband still held off. "Oh we like it as it is. There's always *something*." With which they had approached the door of egress.

"What is there, please?" asked Morris Gedge, not yet opening the door, since he would fain have kept the pair on, and conscious only for a moment after he had spoken that his question was just having for the young man too dreadfully wrong a sound. This personage wondered yet feared, and had evidently for some minutes been putting himself a question; so that, with his preoccupation, the caretaker's words had represented to him inevitably:

"What is there, please, for *me*?" Gedge already knew with it moreover that he wasn't stopping him in time. He had uttered that challenge to show he himself wasn't afraid, and he must have had in consequence, he was subsequently to reflect, a lamentable air of waiting.

The visitor's hand came out. "I hope I may take the liberty——?" What afterwards happened our friend scarcely knew, for it fell into a slight confusion, the confusion of a queer gleam of gold—a sovereign fairly thrust at him; of a quick, almost violent motion on his own part, which, to make the matter worse, might well have sent the money roiling on the floor; and then of marked blushes all round and a sensible embarrassment; producing indeed in turn rather oddly and ever so quickly an increase of communion. It was as if the young man had offered him money to make up to him for having, as it were, led him on, and then, perceiving the mistake, but liking him the better for his refusal, had wanted to obliterate this aggravation of his original wrong. He had done so, presently, while Gedge got the door open, by saying the best thing, he could, and by saying it frankly and gaily. "Luckily it doesn't at all affect the *work*!"

The small town-street, quiet and empty in the summer eventide, stretched to right and left, with a gabled and timbered house or two, and fairly seemed to have cleared itself to congruity with the historic void over which our friends, lingering an instant to converse, looked at each other. The young wife, rather, looked about a moment at all there wasn't to be seen, and then, before Gedge had found a reply to her husband's remark, uttered, evidently in the interest of conciliation, a little question of her own that she tried to make earnest. "It's our unfortunate ignorance, you mean, that doesn't?"

"Unfortunate or fortunate. I like it so," said the husband. "'The play's the thing.' Let the author alone."

Gedge, with his key on his forefinger, leaned against the door-post, took in the stupid little street and was sorry to see them go—they seemed so to abandon him. "That's just what They won't do—nor let *me* do. It›s all I want—to let the author alone. Practically"—he felt himself getting the last of his chance—"there is no author; that is for us to deal with. There are all the immortal people—*in* the work; but there›s nobody else.»

"Yes," said the young man—"that's what it comes to. There should really, to clear the matter up, be no such Person."

"As you say," Gedge returned, "it's what it comes to. There *is* no such Person.»

The evening air listened, in the warm thick midland stillness, while the wife's little cry rang out. "But *wasn't* there——?»

"There was somebody," said Gedge against the door-post. "But They've killed Him. And, dead as He is, They keep it up, They do it over again, They kill Him every day."

He was aware of saying this so grimly—more than he wished—that his companions exchanged a glance and even perhaps looked as if they felt him extravagant. That was really the way Isabel had warned him all the others would be looking if he should talk to Them as he talked to *her*. He liked, however, for that matter, to hear how he should sound when pronounced incapable through deterioration of the brain. "Then if there's no author, if there's nothing to be said but that there isn't anybody," the young woman smilingly asked, "why in the world should there be a house?"

"There shouldn't," said Morris Gedge.

Decidedly, yes, he affected the young man. "Oh, I don't say, mind you, that you should pull it down!"

"Then where would you *go*?" their companion sweetly inquired.

"That's what my wife asks," Gedge returned.

"Then keep it up, keep it up!" And the husband held out his hand.

"That's what my wife says," Gedge went on as he shook it.

The young woman, charming creature, emulated the other visitor; she offered their remarkable friend her handshake. "Then mind your wife."

The poor man faced her gravely. "I would if she were such a wife as you!"

VI

It had made for him, all the same, an immense difference; it had given him an extraordinary lift, so that a certain sweet aftertaste of his freedom might a couple of months later have been suspected of aiding to produce for him another and really a more considerable adventure. It was an absurd way to reason, but he had been, to his imagination, for twenty minutes in good society—that being the term that best described for him the company of people to whom he hadn't to talk, as he phrased it, rot. It was his title to good society that he had, in his doubtless awkward way, affirmed; and the difficulty was just that, having affirmed it, he couldn't take back the affirmation. Few things had happened to him in life, that is few that were agreeable, but at least *this* had, and he wasn›t so constructed that he could go on as if it hadn›t. It was going on as if it had, however, that landed him, alas! in the situation unmistakably marked by a visit from Grant-Jackson late one afternoon toward the end of October. This had been the hour of the call of the young Americans. Every day that hour had come round something of the deep throb of it, the successful secret, woke up; but the two occasions were, of a truth, related only by being so intensely opposed. The secret had been successful in that he had said nothing of it to Isabel, who, occupied in their own quarter while the incident lasted, had neither heard the visitors arrive nor seen them depart. It was on the other hand scarcely successful in guarding itself from indirect betrayals. There were two persons in the world at least who felt as he did; they were persons also who had treated him, benignly, as feeling after *their* style; who had been ready in fact to overflow in gifts as a sign of it, and though they were now off in space they were still with him sufficiently in spirit to make him play, as it were, with the sense of their sympathy. This in turn made him, as he was perfectly aware, more than a shade or two reckless, so that, in his reaction from that gluttony of the public for false facts which had from the first tormented him, he fell into the habit of sailing, as he would have said, too near the wind, or in other words—all in presence of the people—of washing his hands of the legend. He had crossed the line—he knew it; he had struck wild—They drove him to it;

he had substituted, by a succession of uncontrollable profanities, an attitude that couldn't be understood for an attitude that but too evidently *had* been.

This was of course the franker line, only he hadn't taken it, alas! for frankness—hadn't in the least really adopted it at all, but had been simply himself caught up and disposed of by it, hurled by his fate against the bedizened walls of the temple, quite in the way of a priest possessed to excess of the god, or, more vulgarly, that of a blind bull in a china-shop—an animal to which he often compared himself. He had let himself fatally go, in fine, just for irritation, for rage, having, in his predicament, nothing whatever to do with frankness—a luxury reserved for quite other situations. It had always been his view that one lived to learn; he had learned something every hour of his life, though people mostly never knew what, in spite of its having generally been—hadn't it?—at somebody's expense. What he was at present continually learning was the sense of a form of words heretofore so vain—the famous "false position" that had so often helped out a phrase. One used names in that way without knowing what they were worth; then of a sudden, one fine day, their meaning grew bitter in the mouth. This was a truth with the relish of which his fireside hours were occupied, and he was aware of how much it exposed a man to look so perpetually as if something had disagreed with him. The look to be worn at the Birthplace was properly the beatific, and when once it had fairly been missed by those who took it for granted, who indeed paid sixpence for it—like the table-wine in provincial France it was *compris*—one would be sure to have news of the remark.

News accordingly was what Gedge had been expecting—and what he knew, above all, had been expected by his wife, who had a way of sitting at present as with an ear for a certain knock. She didn't watch him, didn't follow him about the house, at the public hours, to spy upon his treachery; and that could touch him even though her averted eyes went through him more than her fixed. Her mistrust was so perfectly expressed by her manner of showing she trusted that he never felt so nervous, never tried so to keep straight, as when she most let him alone. When the crowd thickened and they had of necessity to receive together he tried himself to get off by allowing her as much as possible the word. When people appealed to him he turned to her—and with more of ceremony than their relation warranted: he couldn't help *this* either, if it seemed ironic—as to the person most concerned or most competent. He flattered himself at these moments that no one would have guessed her being his wife; especially as to do her justice, she met his manner with a wonderful grim bravado—grim, so to say, for himself, grim by its outrageous cheerfulness for the simple-minded. The lore she *did* produce for them, the associations of the sacred spot she developed, multiplied, embroidered; the things in short she said and the stupendous way she said them! She wasn't a bit ashamed, since why need virtue be ever ashamed? It was virtue, for it put bread into his mouth—he meanwhile on his side taking it out of hers. He had seen Grant-Jackson on the October day in the Birthplace itself—the right setting of course for such an interview; and what had occurred was that, precisely, when the scene had ended and he had come back to their own sitting-room, the question she put to him for information was: "Have you settled it that I'm to starve?"

She had for a long time said nothing to him so straight—which was but a proof of her real anxiety; the straightness of Grant-Jackson's visit, following on the very slight sinuosity of a note shortly before received from him, made tension show for what it was. By this time, really, however, his decision had been taken; the minutes elapsing between his reappearance at the domestic fireside and his having, from the other threshold, seen Grant-Jackson's broad well-fitted back, the back of a banker and a patriot, move away, had, though few, presented themselves to him as supremely critical. They formed, as it were, the hinge of his door, that door actually ajar so as to show him a possible fate beyond it, but which, with his hand, in a spasm, thus tightening on the knob, he might either open wide or close partly or altogether. He stood at autumn dusk in the little museum that constituted the vestibule of the temple, and there, as with a concentrated push at the crank of a windlass, he brought himself round. The portraits on the walls seemed vaguely to watch for it; it was in their august presence—kept dimly august for the moment by Grant-Jackson's impressive check of his application of a match to the vulgar gas—that the great man had uttered, as if it said all, his "You know, my dear fellow, really——!" He had managed it with the special tact of a fat man, always, when there *was* any, very fine; he had got the most out of the time, the place, the setting, all the little massed admonitions and symbols; confronted there with his victim on the spot that he took occasion to name afresh as, to *his* piety and patriotism, the most sacred on earth, he had given it to be understood that in the first place he was lost in amazement and that in the second he expected a single warning now to suffice. Not to insist too much moreover on the question of gratitude, he would let his remonstrance rest, if need be, solely on the question of taste. *As* a matter of taste alone——!

But he was surely not to be obliged to follow that up. Poor Gedge indeed would have been sorry to oblige him, for he saw it was exactly to the atrocious taste of unthankfulness the allusion was made. When he said he wouldn't dwell on what the fortunate occupant of the post owed him for the stout battle originally fought on his behalf, he simply meant he *would*. That was his tact—which, with everything else that has been mentioned, in the scene, to help, really had the ground to itself. The day *had* been when Gedge couldn›t have thanked him enough—though he had thanked him, he considered, almost fulsomely—and nothing, nothing that he could coherently or reputably name, had happened since then. From the moment he was pulled up, in short, he had no case, and if he exhibited, instead of one, only hot tears in his eyes, the mystic gloom of the temple either prevented his friend from seeing them or rendered it possible that they stood for remorse. He had dried them, with the pads formed by the base of his bony thumbs, before he went in to Isabel. This was the more fortunate as, in spite of her inquiry, prompt and pointed, he but moved about the room looking at her hard. Then he stood before the fire a little with his hands behind him and his coat-tails divided, quite as the person in permanent possession. It was an indication his wife appeared to take in; but she put nevertheless presently another question. "You object to telling me what he said?"

"He said 'You know, my dear fellow, really——!'"

"And is that all?"

"Practically. Except that I'm a thankless beast."

"Well!" she responded, not with dissent.

"You mean that I *am*?"

"Are those the words he used?" she asked with a scruple.

Gedge continued to think. "The words he used were that I give away the Show and that, from several sources, it has come round to Them."

"As of course a baby would have known!" And then as her husband said nothing: "Were *those* the words he used?»

"Absolutely. He couldn't have used better ones."

"Did he call it," Mrs. Gedge inquired, "the 'Show'?"

"Of course he did. The Biggest on Earth."

She winced, looking at him hard—she wondered, but only for a moment. "Well, it *is*."

"Then it's something," Gedge went on, "to have given *that* away. But,» he added, «I›ve taken it back.»

"You mean you've been convinced?"

"I mean I've been scared."

"At last, at last!" she gratefully breathed.

"Oh it was easily done. It was only two words. But here I am."

Her face was now less hard for him. "And what two words?"

"'You know, Mr. Gedge, that it simply won't do.' That was all. But it was the way such a man says them."

"I'm glad then," Mrs. Gedge frankly averred, "that he *is* such a man. How did you ever think it *could* do?»

"Well, it was my critical sense. I didn't ever know I had one—till They came and (by putting me here) waked it up in me. Then I had somehow, don't you see? to live with it; and I seemed to feel that, with one thing and another, giving it time and in the long run, it might, it *ought* to, come out on top of the heap. Now that's where, he says, it simply won't 'do.' So I must put it—I *have* put it—at the bottom.»

"A very good place then for a critical sense!" And Isabel, more placidly now, folded her work. "*If*, that is, you can only keep it there. If it doesn't struggle up again."

"It can't struggle." He was still before the fire, looking round at the warm low room, peaceful in the lamplight, with the hum of the kettle for the ear, with the curtain drawn over the leaded casement, a short moreen curtain artfully chosen by Isabel for the effect of the olden time, its virtue of letting the light within show ruddy to the street. "It's dead," he went on; "I killed it just now."

He really spoke so that she wondered. "Just now?"

"There in the other place—I strangled it, poor thing, in the dark. If you'll go out and see, there must be blood. Which, indeed," he added, "on an altar of sacrifice, is all right. But the place is for ever spattered."

"I don't want to go out and see." She locked her hands over the needlework folded on her knee, and he knew, with her eyes on him, that a look he had seen before was in her face. "You're off your head, you know, my dear, in a way." Then, however, more cheeringly: "It's a good job it hasn't been too late."

"Too late to get it under?"

"Too late for Them to give you the second chance that I thank God you accept."

"Yes, if it *had* been——!» And he looked away as through the ruddy curtain and into the chill street. Then he faced her again. «I›ve scarcely got over my fright yet. I mean,» he went on, «for you."

"And I mean for *you.* Suppose what you had come to announce to me now were that we had *got* the sack. How should I enjoy, do you think, seeing you turn out? Yes, out *there!*" she added as his eyes again moved from their little warm circle to the night of early winter on the other side of the pane, to the rare quick footsteps, to the closed doors, to the curtains drawn like their own, behind which the small flat town, intrinsically dull, was sitting down to supper.

He stiffened himself as he warmed his back; he held up his head, shaking himself a little as if to shake the stoop out of his shoulders, but he had to allow she was right. "What would have become of us?"

"What indeed? We should have begged our bread—or I should be taking in washing."

He was silent a little. "I'm too old. I should have begun sooner."

"Oh God forbid!" she cried.

"The pinch," he pursued, "is that I can do nothing else."

"Nothing whatever!" she agreed with elation.

"Whereas here—if I cultivate it—I perhaps *can* still lie. But I must cultivate it."

"Oh you old dear!" And she got up to kiss him.

"I'll do my best," he said.

VII

"Do you remember us?" the gentleman asked and smiled—with the lady beside him smiling too; speaking so much less as an earnest pilgrim or as a tiresome tourist than as an old acquaintance. It was history repeating itself as Gedge had somehow never expected, with almost everything the same except that the evening was now a mild April-end, except that the visitors had put off mourning and showed all their bravery—besides showing, as he doubtless did himself, though so differently, for a little older; except, above all, that—oh seeing them again suddenly affected him not a bit as the thing he'd have supposed it. "We're in England again and we were near; I've a brother at Oxford with whom we've been spending a day, so that we thought we'd come over." This the young man pleasantly said while our friend took in the queer fact that he must himself seem to them rather coldly to gape. They had come in the same way at the quiet close; another August had passed, and this was the second spring; the Birthplace, given the hour, was about to suspend operations till the morrow; the last lingerer had gone and the fancy of the visitors was once more for a look round by themselves. This represented surely no greater presumption than the terms on which they had last parted with him seemed to warrant; so that if he did inconsequently stare it was just in fact because he was so supremely far from having forgotten them. But the sight of the pair luckily had a double effect, and the first precipitated the second—the second being really his sudden vision that everything perhaps depended for him on his recognising no complication. He must go straight on, since it was what had for more than a year now so handsomely answered; he must brazen it out consistently, since that only was what his dignity was at last reduced to. He mustn't be afraid in one way any more than he had been in another; besides which it came over him to the point of his flushing for it that their visit, in its essence, must have been for himself. It was good society again, and *they* were the same. It wasn›t for him therefore to behave as if he couldn›t meet them.

These deep vibrations, on Gedge's part, were as quick as they were deep; they came in fact all at once, so that his response, his declaration that it was all right—"Oh *rather*; the hour doesn't matter for *you!*"—had hung fire but an instant; and when they were well across the threshold and the door closed behind them, housed in the twilight of the temple, where, as before, the votive offerings glimmered on the walls, he drew the long breath of one who might by a self-betrayal have done something too dreadful. For what had brought them back was indubitably not the glamour of the shrine itself—since he had had a glimpse of their analysis of that quantity; but their critical (not to say their sentimental) interest in the queer case of the priest. Their call was the tribute of curiosity, of sympathy, of a compassion really, as such things went, exquisite—a tribute *to* that queerness which entitled them to the frankest welcome. They had wanted, for the generous wonder of it, to judge how he was getting on, how such a man in such a place *could*; and they had doubtless more than half-expected to see the door opened by somebody who had succeeded him. Well, somebody *had*—only with a strange equivocation; as they would have, poor things, to make out themselves, an embarrassment for which he pitied them. Nothing could have been more odd, but verily it was this troubled vision of their possible bewilderment, and this compunctious view of such a return for their amenity, that practically determined in him his tone. The lapse of the months had but made their name familiar to him; they had on the other occasion inscribed it, among the thousand names, in the current public register, and he had since then, for reasons of his own, reasons of feeling, again and again turned back to it. It was nothing in itself; it told him nothing—"Mr. and Mrs. B. D. Hayes, New York"—one of those American labels that were just like every other American label and that were precisely the most remarkable thing about people reduced to achieving an identity in such other ways. They could be Mr. and Mrs. B. D. Hayes and yet could be, with all presumptions missing—well, what these callers were. It had quickly enough indeed cleared the situation a little further that his friends had absolutely, the other time, as it came back to him, warned him of his original danger, their anxiety about which had been the last note sounded among them. What he was afraid of, with this reminiscence, was that, finding him still safe, they would, the next thing, definitely congratulate him and perhaps even, no less candidly, ask him how he had managed. It was with the sense of nipping some such inquiry in the bud that, losing no time and holding himself with a firm grip, he began on the spot, downstairs, to make plain to them how he had managed. He routed the possibility of the question in short by the assurance of his answer. "Yes, yes, I'm still here; I suppose it *is* in a manner to one›s profit that one does, such as it is, one›s best.» He did his best on the present occasion, did it with the gravest face he had ever worn and a soft serenity that was like a large damp sponge passed over their previous meeting—over everything in it, that is, but the fact of its pleasantness.

"We stand here, you see, in the old living-room, happily still to be reconstructed in the mind's eye, in spite of the havoc of time, which we have fortunately of late years been able to arrest. It was of course rude and humble, but it must have been snug and quaint, and we have at least the pleasure of knowing that the tradition in respect to the features that do remain is delightfully uninterrupted. Across that threshold He habitually passed; through those low windows, in childhood, He peered out into the world that He was to make so much happier by the gift to it of His genius; over the boards of this floor—that is over *some* of them, for we mustn't be carried away!—his little feet often pattered; and the beams of this ceiling (we must really in some places take care of *our* heads!) he endeavoured, in boyish strife, to jump up and touch. It›s not often that in the early home of genius and renown the whole tenor of existence is laid so bare, not often that we are able to retrace, from point to point and from step to step, its connexion with objects, with influences—to build it round again with the little solid facts out of which it sprang. This therefore, I need scarcely remind you, is what makes the small space between these walls—so modest to measurement, so insignificant of aspect—unique on all the earth. *There's nothing like it*," Morris Gedge went on, insisting as solemnly and softly, for his bewildered hearers, as over a pulpit-edge; "there's nothing at all like it anywhere in the world. There's nothing, only reflect, for the combination of greatness and, as we venture to say, of intimacy. You may find elsewhere perhaps absolutely fewer changes, but where shall you find a *Presence* equally diffused, uncontested and undisturbed? Where in particular shall you find, on the part of the abiding spirit, an equally towering eminence? You may find elsewhere eminence of a considerable order, but where shall you find *with* it, don›t you see, changes after all so few and the contemporary element caught so, as it were, in the very fact?» His visitors, at first confounded but gradually spellbound, were still gaping with the universal gape—wondering, he judged, into what strange pleasantry he had been suddenly moved to explode, and yet beginning to see in him an intention beyond a joke, so that they started, at this point, they almost jumped, when, by as rapid a transition, he made, toward the old fireplace, a dash that seemed to illustrate precisely the act of eager catching. "It is in this old chimney-corner, the quaint inglenook of our ancestors—just there in the far angle, where His little stool was placed, and where, I daresay, if we could look close enough, we should find the hearth stone scraped with His little feet—that we see the inconceivable child gazing into the blaze of the old oaken logs and making out there pictures and stories, see Him conning, with curly bent head, His well-worn hornbook, or poring over some scrap of an ancient ballad, some page of some such rudely-bound volume of chronicles as lay, we may be sure, in His father's window-seat."

It was, he even himself felt at this moment, wonderfully done; no auditors, for all his thousands, had ever yet so inspired him. The odd slightly alarmed shyness in the two faces, as if in a drawing-room, in their "good society" exactly, some act incongruous, something grazing the indecent, had abruptly been perpetrated, the painful reality of which stayed itself before coming home—the visible effect on his friends in fine wound him up as to the sense that *they* were worth the trick. It came of itself now—he had got it so by heart; but perhaps really it had never come so well, with the staleness so disguised, the interest so renewed and the clerical unction demanded by the priestly character so successfully distilled. Mr. Hayes of New York had more than once looked at his wife, and Mrs. Hayes of New York had more than once looked at her husband—only, up to now, with a stolen glance, with eyes it hadn't been easy to detach from the remarkable countenance by the aid of which their entertainer held them. At present, however, after an exchange less furtive, they ventured on a sign that they hadn't been appealed to in vain. "Charming, charming, Mr. Gedge!" Mr. Hayes broke out. "We feel that we've caught you in the mood."

His wife hastened to assent—it eased the tension. "It *would* be quite the way; except,» she smiled, «that you›d be too dangerous. You›ve really a genius!"

Gedge looked at her hard, but yielding no inch, even though she touched him there at a point of consciousness that quivered. This was the prodigy for him, and had been, the year through—that he did it all, he found, easily, did it better than he had done anything else in life; with so high and broad an effect, in truth, an inspiration so rich and free, that his poor wife now, literally, had been moved more than once to fresh fear. She had had her bad moments, he knew, after taking the measure of his new direction—moments of readjusted suspicion in which she wondered if he hadn't simply adopted another, a different perversity. There would be more than one fashion of giving away the Show, and wasn't *this* perhaps a question of giving it away by excess? He could dish them by too much romance as well as by too little; she hadn't hitherto fairly grasped that there might *be* too much. It was a way like another, at any rate, of reducing the place to the absurd; which reduction, if he didn›t look out, would reduce *them* again to the prospect of the streets, and this time surely without appeal. It all depended indeed—he knew she knew that—on how much Grant-Jackson and the others, how much the Body, in a word, would take. He knew she knew what he himself held it would take—that he considered no limit could be imputed to the quantity. They simply wanted it piled up, and so did every one else; wherefore if no one reported him as before why were They to be uneasy? It was in consequence of idiots tempted to reason that he had been dealt with before; but as there was now no form of idiocy that he didn't systematically flatter, goading it on really to its *own* private doom, who was ever to pull the string of the guillotine? The axe was in the air—yes; but in a world gorged to satiety there were no revolutions. And it had been vain for Isabel to ask if the other thunder-growl also hadn't come out of the blue. There was actually proof positive that the winds were now at rest. How could they be more so?—he appealed to the receipts. These were golden days—the Show had never so flourished. So he had argued, so he was arguing still—and, it had to be owned, with every appearance in his favour. Yet if he inwardly winced at the tribute to his plausibility rendered by his flushed friends, this was because he felt in it the real ground of his optimism. The charming woman before him acknowledged his "genius" as he himself had had to do. He had been surprised at his facility until he had grown used to it. Whether or no he had, as a fresh menace to his future, found a new perversity, he had found a vocation much older, evidently, than he had at first been prepared to recognise. He had done himself injustice. He liked to be brave because it came so easy; he could measure it off by the yard. It was in the Birthroom, above all, that he continued to do this, having ushered up his companions without, as he was still more elated to feel, the turn of a hair. She might take it as she liked, but he had had the lucidity—all, that is, for his own safety—to meet without the grace of an answer the homage of her beautiful smile. She took it apparently, and her husband took it, but as a part of his odd humour, and they followed him aloft with faces now a little more responsive to the manner in which on *that* spot he would naturally come out. He came out, according to the word of his assured private receipt, «strong.» He missed a little, in truth, the usual round-eyed question from them—the inveterate artless cue with which, from moment to moment, clustered troops had for a year obliged him. Mr. and Mrs. Hayes were from New York, but it was a little like singing, as he had heard one of his Americans once say about something, to a Boston audience. He did none the less what he could, and it was ever his practice to stop still at a certain spot in the room and, after having secured attention by look and gesture, suddenly shoot off: "Here!"

They always understood, the good people—he could fairly love them now for it; they always said breathlessly and unanimously "There?" and stared down at the designated point quite as if some trace of the grand event were still to be made out. This movement produced he again looked round. "Consider it well: *the* spot of earth——!» «Oh but it isn›t *earth!*" the boldest spirit—there was always a boldest—would generally pipe out. Then the guardian of the Birthplace would be truly superior—as if the unfortunate had figured the Immortal coming up, like a potato, through the soil. "I'm not suggesting that He was born on the bare ground. He was born *here!*"—with an uncompromising dig of his heel. "There ought to be a brass, with an inscription, let in." "Into the floor?"—it always came. "Birth and burial: seedtime, summer, autumn!"— that always, with its special right cadence, thanks to his unfailing spring, came too. "Why not as well as into the pavement of the church?—you've *seen* our grand old church?» The former of which questions nobody ever answered— abounding, on the other hand, to make up, in relation to the latter. Mr. and Mrs. Hayes even were at first left dumb by it—not indeed, to do them justice, having uttered the word that called for it. They had uttered no word while he kept the game up, and (though that made it a little more difficult) he could yet stand triumphant before them after he had finished with his flourish. Only then it was that Mr. Hayes of New York broke silence.

"Well, if we wanted to see I think I may say we're quite satisfied. As my wife says, it *would* seem your line." He spoke now, visibly, with more ease, as if a light had come: though he made no joke of it, for a reason that presently appeared. They were coming down the little stair, and it was on the descent that his companion added her word.

"Do you know what we half *did* think——?» And then to her husband: «Is it dreadful to tell him?» They were in the room below, and the young woman, also relieved, expressed the feeling with gaiety. She smiled as before at Morris Gedge, treating him as a person with whom relations were possible, yet remaining just uncertain enough to invoke Mr. Hayes's opinion. "We *have* awfully wanted—from what we had heard.» But she met her husband›s graver face; he was not quite out of the wood. At this she was slightly flurried—but she cut it short. "You must know—don't you?—that, with the crowds who listen to you, we'd have heard."

He looked from one to the other, and once more again, with force, something came over him. They had kept him in mind, they were neither ashamed nor afraid to show it, and it was positively an interest on the part of this charming creature and this keen cautious gentleman, an interest resisting oblivion and surviving separation, that had governed their return. Their other visit had been the brightest thing that had ever happened to him, but this was the gravest; so that at the end of a minute something broke in him and his mask dropped of itself. He chucked, as he would have said, consistency; which, in its extinction, left the tears in his eyes. His smile was therefore queer. "Heard how I'm going it?"

The young man, though still looking at him hard, felt sure, with this, of his own ground. "Of course you're tremendously talked about. You've gone round the world."

"You've heard of me in America?"

"Why almost of nothing else!"

"That was what made us feel——!" Mrs. Hayes contributed.

"That you must see for yourselves?" Again he compared, poor Gedge, their faces. "Do you mean I excite—a—scandal?"

"Dear no! Admiration. You renew so," the young man observed, "the interest."

"Ah there it is!" said Gedge with eyes of adventure that seemed to rest beyond the Atlantic.

"They listen, month after month, when they're out here, as you must have seen; then they go home and talk. But they sing your praise."

Our friend could scarce take it in. "Over *there*!"

"Over there. I think you must be even in the papers."

"Without abuse?"

"Oh we don't abuse every one."

Mrs. Hayes, in her beauty, it was clear, stretched the point. "They rave about you."

"Then they *don't* know?»

"Nobody knows," the young man declared; "it wasn't any one's knowledge, at any rate, that made us uneasy."

"It was your own? I mean your own sense?"

"Well, call it that. We remembered, and we wondered what had happened. So," Mr. Hayes now frankly laughed, "we came to see."

Gedge stared through his film of tears. "Came from America to see *me*?"

"Oh a part of the way. But we wouldn't, in England, have missed you."

"And now we *haven't!*" the young woman soothingly added.

Gedge still could only gape at the candour of the tribute. But he tried to meet them—it was what was least poor for him—in their own key. "Well, how do you like it?"

Mrs. Hayes, he thought—if their answer were important—laughed a little nervously. "Oh you see."

Once more he looked from one to the other. "It's too beastly easy, you know."

Her husband raised his eyebrows. "You conceal your art. The emotion—yes; that must be easy; the general tone must flow. But about your facts—you've so many: how do you get *them* through?»

Gedge wondered. "You think I get too many——?"

At this they were amused together. "That's just what we came to see!"

"Well, you know, I've felt my way; I've gone step by step; you wouldn't believe how I've tried it on. *This*—where you see me—is where I've come out." After which, as they said nothing: "You hadn't thought I *could* come out?»

Again they just waited, but the husband spoke: "Are you so awfully sure you are out?"

Gedge drew himself up in the manner of his moments of emotion, almost conscious even that, with his sloping shoulders, his long lean neck and his nose so prominent in proportion to other matters, he resembled the more a giraffe. It was now at last he really caught on. "I *may* be in danger again—and the danger is what has moved you? Oh!» the poor man fairly moaned. His appreciation of it quite weakened him, yet he pulled himself together. "You've your view of my danger?"

It was wondrous how, with that note definitely sounded, the air was cleared. Lucid Mr. Hayes, at the end of a minute, had put the thing in a nutshell. "I don't know what you'll think of us—for being so beastly curious."

"I think," poor Gedge grimaced, "you're only too beastly kind."

"It's all your own fault," his friend returned, "for presenting us (who are not idiots, say) with so striking a picture of a crisis. At our other visit, you remember," he smiled, "you created an anxiety for the opposite reason. Therefore if *this* should again be a crisis for you, you›d really give us the case with an ideal completeness.»

"You make me wish," said Morris Gedge, "that it might be one."

"Well, don't try—for our amusement—to bring one on. I don't see, you know, how you can have much margin. Take care—take care."

Gedge did it pensive justice. "Yes, that was what you said a year ago. You did me the honour to be uneasy—as my wife was."

Which determined on the young woman's part an immediate question. "May I ask then if Mrs. Gedge is now at rest?"

"No—since you do ask. *She* fears at least that I go too far; she doesn›t believe in my margin. You see we *had* our scare after your visit. They came down."

His friends were all interest. "Ah! They came down?"

"Heavy. They brought *me* down. That›s *why*—"

"Why you *are* down?» Mrs. Hayes sweetly demanded.

"Ah but my dear man," her husband interposed, "you're not down; you're *up*! You're only up a different tree, but you're up at the tip-top."

"You mean I take it too high?"

"That's exactly the question," the young man answered; "and the possibility, as matching your first danger, is just what we felt we couldn't, if you didn't mind, miss the measure of."

Gedge gazed at him. "I feel that I know what you at bottom *hoped*."

"We at bottom 'hope,' surely, that you're all right?"

"In spite of the fool it makes of every one?"

Mr. Hayes of New York smiled. "Say *because* of that. We only ask to believe every one *is* a fool!»

"Only you haven't been, without reassurance, able to imagine fools of the size that my case demands?" And Gedge had a pause while, as if on the chance of some proof, his companion waited. "Well, I won't pretend to you that your anxiety hasn't made me, doesn't threaten to make me, a bit nervous; though I don't quite understand it if, as you say, people but rave about me."

"Oh *that* report was from the other side; people in our country so very easily rave. You›ve seen small children laugh to shrieks when tickled in a new place. So there are amiable millions with us who are but small shrieking children. They perpetually present new places for the tickler. What we've seen in further lights," Mr. Hayes good-humouredly pursued, "is your people *here*—the Committee, the Board, or whatever the powers to whom you're responsible."

"Call them my friend Grant-Jackson then—my original backer, though I admit for that reason perhaps my most formidable critic. It's with him practically I deal; or rather it's by him I'm dealt with—*was* dealt with before. I stand or fall by him. But he has given me my head.»

"Mayn't he then want you," Mrs. Hayes inquired, "just to show as flagrantly running away?"

"Of course—I see what you mean. I'm riding, blindly, for a fall, and They're watching (to be tender of me!) for the smash that may come of itself. It's Machiavellic—but everything's possible. And what did you just now mean," Gedge asked—"especially if you've only heard of my prosperity—by your 'further lights'?"

His friends for an instant looked embarrassed, but Mr. Hayes came to the point. "We've heard of your prosperity, but we've also, remember, within a few minutes, heard *you*."

"I was determined you *should*," said Gedge. "I'm good then—but I overdo?" His strained grin was still sceptical.

Thus challenged, at any rate, his visitor pronounced. "Well, if you don't; if at the end of six months more it's clear that you haven't overdone; then, *then*——"

"Then what?"

"Then it's great."

"But it *is* great—greater than anything of the sort ever was. I overdo, thank goodness, yes; or I would if it were a thing you *could*."

"Oh well, if there's *proof* that you can›t——!» With which and an expressive gesture Mr. Hayes threw up his fears.

His wife, however, for a moment seemed unable to let them go. "Don't They want then *any* truth?—none even for the mere look of it?»

"The look of it," said Morris Gedge, "is what I give!"

It made them, the others, exchange a look of their own. Then she smiled. "Oh, well, if they think so——!"

"You at least don't? You're like my wife—which indeed, I remember," Gedge added, "is a similarity I expressed a year ago the wish for! At any rate I frighten *her*."

The young husband, with an "Ah wives are terrible!" smoothed it over, and their visit would have failed of further excuse had not at this instant a movement at the other end of the room suddenly engaged them. The evening had so nearly closed in, though Gedge, in the course of their talk, had lighted the lamp nearest them, that they had not distinguished, in connexion with the opening of the door of communication to the warden's lodge, the appearance of another person, an eager woman who in her impatience had barely paused before advancing. Mrs. Gedge—her identity took but a few seconds to become vivid—was upon them, and she had not been too late for Mr. Hayes's last remark. Gedge saw at once that she had come with news; no need even, for that certitude, of her quick retort to the words in the air—"You may say as well, sir, that they're often, poor wives, terrified!" She knew nothing of the friends whom, at so unnatural an hour, he was showing about; but there was no livelier sign for him that this didn't matter than the possibility with which she intensely charged her "Grant-Jackson, to see you at once!"—letting it, so to speak, fly in his face.

"He has been with you?"

"Only a minute—he's there. But it's you he wants to see."

He looked at the others. "And what does he want, dear?"

"God knows! There it is. It's his horrid hour—it *was* that other time."

She had nervously turned to the others, overflowing to them, in her dismay, for all their strangeness—quite, as he said to himself, like a woman of the people. She was the bareheaded good wife talking in the street about the row in the house, and it was in this character that he instantly introduced her: "My dear doubting wife, who will do her best to entertain you while I wait upon our friend." And he explained to her as he could his now protesting companions—"Mr. and Mrs. Hayes of New York, who have been here before." He knew, without knowing why, that her announcement chilled him; he failed at least to see why it should chill him so much. His good friends had themselves been visibly affected by it, and heaven knew that the depths of brooding fancy in him were easily stirred by contact. If they had wanted a crisis they accordingly had found one, albeit they had already asked leave to retire before it. This he wouldn't have. "Ah no, you must really see!"

"But we shan't be able to bear it, you know," said the young woman, "if it *is* to turn you out.»

Her crudity attested her sincerity, and it was the latter, doubtless, that instantly held Mrs. Gedge. "It *is* to turn us out.»

"Has he told you that, madam?" Mr. Hayes inquired of her—it being wondrous how the breath of doom had drawn them together.

"No, not told me; but there's something in him there—I mean in his awful manner—that matches too well with other things. We've seen," said the poor pale lady, "other things enough."

The young woman almost clutched her. "Is his manner very awful?"

"It's simply the manner," Gedge interposed, "of a very great man."

"Well, very great men," said his wife, "are very awful things."

"It's exactly," he laughed, "what we're finding out! But I mustn't keep him waiting. Our friends here," he went on, "are directly interested. You mustn't, mind you, let them go until we know."

Mr. Hayes, however, held him; he found himself stayed. "We're so directly interested that I want you to understand this. If anything happens——"

"Yes?" said Gedge, all gentle as he faltered.

"Well, *we* must set you up.»

Mrs. Hayes quickly abounded. "Oh *do* come to us!»

Again he could but take them in. They were really wonderful folk. And with it all but Mr. and Mrs. Hayes! It affected even Isabel through her alarm; though the balm, in a manner, seemed to foretell the wound. He had reached the threshold of his own quarters; he stood there as at the door of the chamber of judgement. But he laughed; at least he could be gallant in going up for sentence. "Very good then—I'll come to you!"

This was very well, but it didn't prevent his heart, a minute later, at the end of the passage, from thumping with beats he could count. He had paused again before going in; on the other side of this second door his poor future was to be let loose at him. It was broken, at best, and spiritless, but wasn't Grant-Jackson there like a beast-tamer in a cage, all tights and spangles and circus attitudes, to give it a cut with the smart official whip and make it spring at him? It was during this moment that he fully measured the effect for his nerves of the impression made on his so oddly earnest friends—whose earnestness he verily, in the spasm of this last effort, came within an ace of resenting. They had upset him by contact; he was afraid literally of meeting his doom on his knees; it wouldn't have taken much more, he absolutely felt, to make him approach with his forehead in the dust the great man whose wrath was to be averted. Mr. and Mrs. Hayes of New York had brought tears to his eyes, but was it to be reserved for Grant-Jackson to make him cry like a baby? He wished, yes, while he palpitated, that Mr. and Mrs. Hayes of New York hadn't had such an eccentricity of interest, for it seemed somehow to come from *them* that he was going so fast to pieces. Before he turned the knob of the door, however, he had another queer instant; making out that it had been, strictly, his case that was interesting, his funny power, however accidental, to show as in a picture the attitude of others—not his poor pale personality. It was this latter quantity, none the less, that was marching to execution. It is to our friend's credit that he *believed*, as he prepared to turn the knob, that he was going to be hanged; and it's certainly not less to his credit that his wife, on the chance, had his supreme thought. Here it was that—possibly with his last articulate breath—he thanked his stars, such as they were, for Mr. and Mrs. Hayes of New York. At least they would take care of her.

They were doing that certainly with some success when he returned to them ten minutes later. She sat between them in the beautified Birthplace, and he couldn't have been sure afterwards that each wasn't holding her hand. The three together had at any rate the effect of recalling to him—it was too whimsical—some picture, a sentimental print, seen and admired in his youth, a "Waiting for the Verdict," a "Counting the Hours," or something of that sort; humble respectability in suspense about humble innocence. He didn't know how he himself looked, and he didn't care; the great thing was that he wasn't crying—though he might have been; the glitter in his eyes was assuredly dry, though that there *was* a glitter, or something slightly to bewilder, the faces of the others as they rose to meet him sufficiently proved. His wife's eyes pierced his own, but it was Mrs. Hayes of New York who spoke. "*Was* it then for that——?»

He only looked at them at first—he felt he might now enjoy it. "Yes, it was for 'that.' I mean it was about the way I've been going on. He came to speak of it."

"And he's gone?" Mr. Hayes permitted himself to inquire.

"He's gone."

"It's over?" Isabel hoarsely asked.

"It's over."

"Then we go?"

This it was that he enjoyed. "No, my dear; we stay."

There was fairly a triple gasp; relief took time to operate. "Then why did he come?"

"In the fulness of his kind heart and of *Their* discussed and decreed satisfaction. To express Their sense——!»

Mr. Hayes broke into a laugh, but his wife wanted to know. "Of the grand work you're doing?"

"Of the way I polish it off. They're most handsome about it. The receipts, it appears, speak——"

He was nursing his effect; Isabel intently watched him and the others hung on his lips. "Yes, speak——?"

"Well, volumes. They tell the truth."

At this Mr. Hayes laughed again. "Oh *they* at least do?»

Near him thus once more Gedge knew their intelligence as one—which was so good a consciousness to get back that his tension now relaxed as by the snap of a spring and he felt his old face at ease. "So you can't say," he continued, "that we don't want it."

"I bow to it," the young man smiled. "It's what I said then. It's *great.*"

"It's great," said Morris Gedge. "It couldn't be greater."

His wife still watched him; her irony hung behind. "Then we're just as we were?"

"No, not as we were."

She jumped at it. "Better?"

"Better. They give us a rise."

"Of income?"

"Of our sweet little stipend—by a vote of the Committee. That's what, as Chairman, he came to announce."

The very echoes of the Birthplace were themselves, for the instant, hushed; the warden's three companions showed in the conscious air a struggle for their own breath. But Isabel, almost with a shriek, was the first to recover hers. "They double us?"

"Well—call it that. 'In recognition.' There you are." Isabel uttered another sound—but this time inarticulate; partly because Mrs. Hayes of New York had already jumped at her to kiss her. Mr. Hayes meanwhile, as with too much to say, but put out his hand, which our friend took in silence. So Gedge had the last word. "And there *you* are!»

9 789357 271608